Aisha
and the turtle

Barbara Steinbauer-Grötsch

with illustrations by Ines A Landmesser

Published with the support
and encouragement of

Published by Motivate Publishing

DUBAI: PO Box 2331, Dubai, UAE
Tel: 04 282 4060, Fax: 04 282 4436
e-mail: motivate@emirates.net.ae

ABU DHABI: PO Box 43072, Abu Dhabi, UAE
Tel/Fax: 02 627 1666

LONDON: Stewart's Court, 220 Stewart's Road,
London SW8 4UD
Tel: (+44 207) 627 2481, fax: (+44 207) 720 3158

Directors:
Obaid Humaid Al Tayer
Ian Fairservice

First Published 2000
Reprinted 2002
© Motivate Publishing 2000

ISBN 1 86063 116 9

British Library Cataloguing-in-Publication Data. A catalogue
record for this book is available from the British Library.

Printed by Rashid Printers & Stationers LLC, Ajman

For our daughters

This is Aisha. She lives in the Arabian Gulf, a beautiful stretch of land in the Middle East. Aisha's aunts and uncles have moved to the city but her house still stands in a small village way up north, where the ocean and mountains almost touch.

Arabian Gulf

Gulf of Oman

Aisha loves the sea. She also loves seashells and has an unusual hobby: drawing them. At night, before she goes to sleep, she studies her drawings. Many questions go through her head. Are shells able to see? What do they eat? And do they ever sleep? She asks her mother and father – and even her grandmother – but nobody can answer her questions.

Every weekend Aisha and her family spend an afternoon at the beach. Her brothers play ball and her mother takes care of Aisha's little sister. Aisha has only one thing on her mind.

"I want to look for seashells to draw," she says.

"What on earth is so exciting about them?" her father grumbles as he lights the barbecue.

"Do not go too far away," her mother warns her. "We will be eating soon. And keep away from the ocean."

"Yes mother." And off she goes, clutching her drawing book.

The sea is calm. "Don't go too far away!" Her mother's words echo in Aisha's head. Then she thinks of the shells again. "Perhaps I will find a special one to draw today."

With her head down and eyes scanning the sand, Aisha walks on and on without finding any nice shells.

Disappointed and tired, she sits on the sand and gazes out to sea. The waves break softly. Splish-splash, splish-splash, splish-splash. Aisha becomes sleepy. "Don't go too far."

She closes her eyes . . .

Aisha dreams she is walking along the beach. Suddenly, she discovers something shining in the sand. As she bends down to look closer, a deep voice resounds.

"What are you doing here?" Two dark eyes stare at her. In front of her sits a huge turtle.

"I . . . I . . . am looking for seashells to draw," Aisha stutters.

"Why don't you pick that up instead?" asks the turtle, pointing at a plastic bag.

"But that's useless stuff. I don't want that."

"We sea animals don't want it either! It makes us sick, you know." The turtle already sounds a lot friendlier.

"What's your name?"

"Aisha!"

"I'm Um-Sulhufa, the green turtle. Nice meeting you, Aisha. So, have you found any seashells to draw?"

Aisha shakes her head sadly. "No, nothing at all."

"Why don't you look in the ocean?"

"I mustn't swim in the sea by myself," Aisha answers.

"Well, then, climb on my back, I'll show you."

"You mean, I should . . ." Aisha stutters.

"Yes. Or are you afraid?" asks Um-Sulhufa with a gentle smile.

"No."

"Then come. You will like it down there."

Aisha climbs on to Um-Sulhufa's shell. Slowly, the turtle slides into another world, full of wonders and surprises.

Fluorescent fish bustle in the waves, a jellyfish floats by, and shell-fish in the most beautiful shapes and sizes lie on the coral reef.

Aisha is thrilled. "Look at all these mussels!"

"Only some of them are mussels. They form part of the class of bivalves. Another big class is called gastropods. Snails belong to it."

"What's the difference between the two?"

"For one thing, mussels have two shells while snails only have one."

"Can I have a closer look so that I can draw them later?"

"Sure. But remember that they are all alive. So be gentle with them and don't take any home!"

While Aisha studies the shells, many questions go through her head. "Say, Um-Sulhufa, can snails actually see?"

"Yes, snails have eyes."

"Do they sleep?"

"Well, they rest."

"And what do they eat?"

"Many eat plankton," answers Um-Sulhufa. "Plankton consists of animals and plants that float in the water."

"But I see nothing at all."

"Plankton is very, very tiny. You can't see it with the naked eye but it's still everywhere, surrounding us.

"But not all shelled animals eat it. Some feed on algae. Others – such as several species of cone shell – use a poison to paralyse their prey before they eat it."

"Ugh, I wouldn't want to touch one of them," Aisha replies.

"You'd better not. Talking about food, let's have lunch. I'm starved."

Carefully, Aisha puts the shelled creatures back. Then Um-Sulhufa dives and makes her way towards a field of strange vegetation which sways gently to the rhythm of the waves.

"What kind of plants are they?" Aisha asks curiously.

"That's sea grass, my favourite food," Um-Sulhufa explains

as she chews on a stem. "Mmmm. Do you want to try it?"

"Thanks, but I . . . I'm not hungry," Aisha replies quickly. No matter how beautiful the sea grass is, she does not want to eat it!

She opens her sketch book and starts to draw.

Once Um-Sulhufa has eaten, she and Aisha return to the reef.

"How do you know so many things, Um-Sulhufa?"

"My turtle family has been living here in the sea for more than 120 million years."

"Wow, that's a long time, isn't it? How old are you?"

"I'm 95."

"Then you're even older than my grandmother," Aisha exclaims. "And she is very old."

Suddenly, a big octopus appears from behind an outcrop in the reef. Aisha is terrified.

"Um-Sulhufa, let's go, quick! A monster is coming!"

"Don't worry, that's Okty, an old friend of mine.
Hello Okty. This is my friend Aisha."

Okty stretches one of his tentacles towards her.

"Welcome to our home, Aisha."

Aisha cautiously takes the tentacle in her hand.
The little suction caps have a sticky feel to them.

"Aisha is interested in sea life," explains Um-Sulhufa.

"Especially shells," Aisha adds. "I draw shells."

"Well then, come along. I might have something
special for you."

Um-Sulhufa and Aisha follow Okty to the edge of a small gully. He sinks down towards its bottom, carefully picks up something white, and brings it to show Aisha. It is a beautiful shell as big as her hand.

"Be gentle . . ."

"Don't worry, I won't hurt it. I know it's alive," replies Aisha.

"You're a clever girl, Aisha," says Okty, smiling.

"She sure is," Um-Sulhufa agrees.

Thrilled, Aisha draws the shell. "Thank you, Okty."

"My pleasure. Well, I have to move on. Bye Aisha! Go well."

"You too! And many thanks for showing me . . . what is it actually? A mussel or a snail?"

"A snail, *Murex scolopax*," calls Okty.

And then he's gone.

"Well, I think it's time to take you back," says Um-Sulhufa. "Otherwise your parents will be worried."

"Will you take me down another time?"

"Anytime you like," replies the old turtle.

Aisha places the beautiful snail back where Okty found it and they move up towards the sunlight. Suddenly Um-Sulhufa stops. She has spotted a young turtle going after something floating on the surface.

"Tevo! Stop! Don't eat it!" shouts Um-Sulhufa.

But Tevo does not seem to hear her.

"We must help him." Um-Sulhufa swims up to the object.

"Quickly, Aisha, get it!"

Aisha tries to grab it but Tevo already has a piece in his mouth.

"Pull harder, Aisha!"

"Hey, that jellyfish belongs to me," Tevo snaps angrily.

"That's not a jellyfish, it's a plastic bag," says Aisha.

Finally she manages to pull it away.

"If you eat it, you could die," Um-Sulhufa points out sternly and wisely.

"Why?" the young turtle asks naively.

"Because we turtles can't digest plastic — it blocks our insides. . . ."

"Gee, I didn't know that," answers Tevo, meekly.

"From now on I will look twice before I munch something!" With a humble nod, he swims away.

"That was a close call," Aisha says, relieved.

"Indeed," Um-Sulhufa replies. "Now, what shall we do with the bag?"

Aisha thinks for a moment. "I will take it home. Then no turtle can eat it."

Aisha puts her drawing book in the bag and they continue their journey. Then, out of nowhere, something drops on top of them.

"Um-Sulhufa, what on earth is happening?"

"We are caught in a fishing net!" Um-Sulhufa tries desperately to free herself, but the harder she tries, the more tangled she becomes.

"Hold on, I'll help you," Aisha shouts. As she tries to loosen the net, the bag floats away from her hand. The net pulls tighter around them. Aisha is tossed and turned.

"Aisha! Aisha!"

She blinks, opens her eyes and sees her mother.

"Is everything okay, *habibti*?"

Aisha moves her hands and feet. Relieved, she says:
"Thank goodness, they didn't catch us."

"What?"

"Um-Sulhufa wanted to bring me home and all of a sudden
there was this big fishing net all around us!"

"Who on earth is Um-Sulhufa?"

"A turtle. She took me down to the sea."

"You were dreaming, *habibti*?"

"No, I was down there." Aisha motions towards the sea.

"I saw everything – mussels, snails, plankton and sea grass."

She is all excited now. "And, you know, turtles mustn't eat plastic bags because then . . ."

"Aisha, you really have a vivid imagination." Her mother shakes her head in disbelief.

Didn't I tell you not to go too far away?"

"But I was only looking for shells to draw."

"You and your shells. Come along now.

"Did you find anything after all?" her mother asks on their way back.

"No," Aisha answers sadly, noticing that her drawing book is missing.

"Don't be sad, you may have more luck next time."

They walk together in silence. Suddenly, Aisha discovers a plastic bag on the beach. She picks it up. It's heavy. As she takes a closer look, she can hardly believe her eyes. Inside is a notebook exactly like hers. She opens it. It is filled with drawings of shells. The most beautiful is a sketch of a big white *Murex scolopax*! She looks out to the sea.

There, in the distance, is a black dot!

She looks more closely. Is that Um-Sulhufa waving at her?

My favourite family
picture on the beach

Things I can do to protect
Um-Sulhufa, Tevo and their friends

_____

_____

_____

_____

_____

_____

_____

_____

_____

This is Dr Saif Al Ghais, who
is working hard to protect turtles
like Um-Sulhufa and Tevo. Dr Saif
works for the Environmental
Research and Wildlife Development
Agency of the UAE. Part of his work
on turtles is sponsored by a large
energy company called Shell.